化石超進化

SPECTROBES

FIRST CONTACT

By Ned Lerr
Based on the Disney Interactive Studios videogame
Original concept by Fil Barlow and Helen Maier

Disney

New

Printed in the United States of America

First Edition
1 3 5 7 9 10 8 6 4 2

Library of Congress Catalog Card Number: 2008906911

ISBN 978-1-4231-0809-2

Visit disneybooks.com

FIRST CONTACT

A long time ago in the Nanairo Galaxy, men roamed the planets in perfect harmony with a rare species known as the Spectrobes: mysterious beings that harness light energy to unleash amazing powers. But that harmony would eventually be lost. The Krawl—an evil force that cannot stand light—appeared in the Nanairo Galaxy and wreaked havoc throughout the planets. The Spectrobes jumped into action and the Krawl were finally beaten, but the fight proved too great, even for the Spectrobes. For reasons unknown, the Spectrobes were fossilized and scattered to surrounding planets where they buried themselves deep in the grounds. All was peaceful, but the peace would not last for long. Now, deep in the blackness of space, thousands of vortexes filled with Krawl are on their way back to the Nanairo Galaxy. . . .

PROLOGUE

The darkness was complete.

One moment it had been a beautiful day on Geneea, a small planet in the Meena system. The wind gently rustled the buds of the qentla trees as sunlight dappled the deep yellow of the sponsolo grasses just coming into bloom. Herds of young vinxol grazed idly on patches of plaed, lowing occasionally. The next moment, the vortex appeared, and minutes later, all that had defined Geneea was gone without a trace.

The Krawl had arrived.

CHAPTER ONE

"*R*allen. *Rallen*. Ral-len!"

Jeena stared at her partner, who seemed oblivious to her calls. He was *supposed* to be using the computer to work up the most efficient way to use a planet's gravitational force to slingshot a ship low on fuel into escape velocity. Instead, he was leaning back in his chair, his feet up on the console; and judging by the smile on his boyish face, he seemed to be playing a game of cavball. A lock of his floppy orange hair dropped into his eyes and he brushed it back, not looking away from the screen for a moment.

Jeena growled softly to herself, then looked around for something to throw. Her own hand-held computer was the right size but too hard. And, besides, it was probably a bit too fragile. Jeena briefly considered her shoe but then her eyes landed on her half-eaten jaxsin fruit. Perfect!

"Hey!" Rallen yelled as the piece of fruit bounced off the back of his head. He looked up at the ceiling, then around for whatever had just hit him. He saw the jaxsin on the floor—the only object out of place in the otherwise pristine environment—and turned to glare at Jeena. "If you wanted my attention, you could have just called me."

Jeena opened her mouth to point out that that was exactly what she had been doing, but then closed it with a snap. She and Rallen had only been partners for the Nanairo Planetary Patrol for a few weeks and were still getting to know each other. But in that short period, she'd already learned to recognize when it was pretty much pointless to argue with him—which seemed to be most of the time. She shook her head as Rallen picked up the jaxsin fruit and took a bite without even bothering to peel back the skin.

Jeena ran a hand through her long pink hair. She took two deep breaths and then, with great restraint, asked, "So, are you nearly done playing with that?"

Rallen grinned. "Yeah, just about. Why, hoping for a turn? Or I could show you the mod you need to be able to access cavball on your own kaylee. It's so simple even someone like you should be able to handle it."

This time Jeena counted to five before replying. "Not exactly. I was just wondering if you were going to do any actual work today."

Rallen tried to look hurt. "Hey, this *is* work. I'm . . ." His eyes narrowed as he tried to find a way to convince Jeena that he wasn't goofing off. "It's . . . you know, considered from a certain point of view, it could be argued that . . . uh . . . the strategies involved have a cumulative effect and . . . I . . ."

Jeena knew better. "Uh-huh," she said, turning her attention back to her own kaylee; she was nearly done mapping the coordinates of the Nanairo system's most eminent threats. These were statistics that were easily available elsewhere, but command thought having its officers do basic work like this kept them more involved personally; the officers got a better feel for hot spots and the general lay of the land. It was not, Jeena had to admit, the most fascinating job ever, but she took great pride in doing it anyway. Besides, Jeena believed wholeheartedly in accumulating as much knowledge as possible in order to be as prepared as she could be. Being able to predict precisely where the highest arrest rate on the planet of Ziba occurred could just save lives.

Jeena recognized that there was no point in saying any of this to Rallen. There was no getting through to him.

"I see you've already finished your analysis, Rallen," a voice called out.

Jeena and Rallen both spun around to see Commander Grant, silver-haired and stern-faced, standing in the doorway. Jeena restrained a smile. She might not be able to get through to Rallen, but there was at least one person who could, and that person had just caught her partner goofing off.

"Commander!" Rallen was on his feet in an instant. "I was just—"

"—counting on your partner to pick up your slack?" Grant interrupted in his oddly casual yet firm manner; neither of the partners had ever encountered anyone quite like him.

"Sir?" Rallen stalled for time. "This is—"

"—Nanairo Planetary Patrol Headquarters located on planet Kollin, where we do our *jobs* when on duty. Such as now."

Rallen started to defend himself, but since he'd pretty much been caught red-handed, he decided it might not be the wisest course of action. "Yes, sir."

Commander Grant nodded. "Both of you suit up."

"Sir?" Jeena asked. "We're not scheduled to start patrol for half an hour."

"I'm aware of that. I want you in the air *now*. Are you questioning my orders?"

Jeena blanched. "No, sir!"

Commander Grant stared at both of them. Hard. "Good. I want you to patrol the area of the planet Daichi. We've just received some very strange readings from there, especially near Tabletop Mountain. The readings came in a few minutes ago, so get going."

"Yes, sir," they said in unison. Rallen was out the door in a flash, but Commander Grant noticed that Jeena moved more deliberately. It was obvious to him that Rallen could potentially be trouble and that Jeena was strictly by the book. Grant couldn't help but wonder if her slight hesitation wasn't her subtle way of asserting her own independence.

"Wait one moment, Jeena" he said. "I want to have a word with you." Jeena stepped out immediately and stood at attention, arms straight down at her sides. Her line of vision was just above the commander's eyes; she stared directly into his slate-gray hair, as she had been taught at the academy. "At ease," he ordered.

Jeena let out the breath she had been holding, relaxed, and clasped her hands behind her back. Commander Grant sighed and brushed some lint off his dark blue uniform, the color signifying his high rank among the NPP. "I know being a Nanairo Planetary Patrol officer isn't exactly the easiest task in the world—but I think you'd agree it's worth the difficulties?"

Jeena smiled slightly. "Yes, sir."

"Good. I'm glad you think so. I also know Rallen isn't the easiest partner in the fleet." Commander Grant paused to see if Jeena would reply. When she said nothing, Grant's eyes narrowed slightly. "I've been here a long time, and I've seen his type before. Some newer officers have trouble focusing on the less exciting tasks more experienced officers recognize are not only necessary, but could save lives: theirs, their

partners', and civilians'. Such officers either learn that or they don't last long. I'm willing to cut Rallen a bit of slack . . . for now."

Commander Grant put a hand on Jeena's shoulder. "So I'm asking you to look out for him. He's an outstanding pilot, one of the most naturally gifted we've ever seen. *But* he's still not quite as good as he thinks he is. And being a brilliant pilot isn't always enough."

Jeena's eyes met Grant's. "I promise to do my best as a partner to Rallen and live up to the standards of the Nanairo Planetary Patrol.

11

And I promise to keep an eye out for him as well."

Commander Grant smiled. "Thank you, Jeena. Though today's patrol may not give you any worries or threats, one day you will be called upon to show your courage, bravery, and dedication. Now go."

And with that, Jeena was off to patrol with her partner.

CHAPTER TWO

*T*he route Commander Grant had specified took Rallen and Jeena right into the heart of an asteroid belt. Huge chunks of rock hurtled past the ship on either side. In the pilot's seat, Rallen grinned, enjoying the challenge. He banked the craft sharply, flying almost on one wingtip, narrowly avoiding a craggy boulder that could have easily pulverized the ship with the slightest touch.

Jeena tried to keep quiet as she watched the

monitors in her navigator's seat. She kept replaying Commander Grant's words in her head. She thought about everything she'd learned at the academy and about being a good partner. There had been a class devoted specifically to the topic, and while Jeena had gotten the highest marks—of course—she found it perhaps the least interesting lesson of her entire training program. Nevertheless, she had recognized at the time that some of its lessons might come in handy—like now.

But she only had so much patience. Rallen was zipping the ship back and forth between asteroids, gunning the engine for more speed, almost as if he were making a game of it.

"We're patrolling, not racing, Rallen," Jeena said.

Rallen nonchalantly glanced over at Jeena and shrugged. "A pilot's got to keep his skills sharp."

Jeena shook her head. "Oh, brother."

"I got news for you." Rallen grinned. "I'm not your brother, I'm your partner. Which means, Jeena, you won the lottery."

"Yeah, right," she replied, punching a few buttons with a little more force than was really necessary. Their fuel supply was fine, and the atmosphere was stable. They'd left HQ on Kollin only a few minutes before, so it was unlikely that either of those things would have changed at all. But it gave her something to do other than look at her partner's cocky expression.

"Hey," Rallen said, his voice suddenly serious. "We've got a distress signal."

Jeena looked up. Sure enough, there was a red-alert symbol flashing on the screen.

She immediately began running a trace. "Origin is nearby—looks like it's in the vicinity of Daichi. It's . . . it's coming from the planet's surface."

"Looks like Commander Grant was right," Rallen responded, excitedly tightening his grip on the controls. "Let's go."

But Jeena held up a hand. "Not without authorization from Command," she protested.

Rallen muttered in irritation and folded his arms. Jeena ignored him.

"Commander," she said into the telecom as calmly as she could. "We've . . . we've got a type-three distress signal."

Commander Grant's steely visage appeared. "Yes, we're aware of it. Go to the site and investigate. Report back to me . . ." The commander's gaze flicked to the side. ". . . and to me alone. Oh, and be careful of the—"

There was a burst of static. Commander Grant's image faded out and then back in, but his words were barely audible.

Jeena leaned over the telecom, twisting the controls and trying for a clearer channel.

"Commander, we didn't get your last . . . Retransmit, please. Commander?"

There was nothing but silence from command and a telescreen full of static. Jeena shook her head. "Rallen, this is weird. I'm getting interference. I've never known the telecom to—"

Jeena broke off as she saw Rallen's eyes widen. Turning to follow his gaze, she saw a spinning, churning, swirling mass of some type of black substance directly in front of the ship. It was almost as if a whirlpool had developed in the middle of space. "Whoa," Jeena breathed.

Her heart was in her throat as Rallen piloted the ship directly above the swirling vortex. Whatever it was, it was vast . . . and dangerous. Streaks of lightning flashed in every direction while pulses of light came from within the mysterious whirlpool.

The ship's alarms began to clang: the monitors

had picked up the presence of other spaceborne objects near the ship. Up from the brilliant depths of the vortex shot dozens of the strangest things Rallen and Jeena had ever seen. Were they spacecraft? Creatures? It was impossible to tell. They looked like small cyclones swirling and spinning out of the larger whirlpool. Jeena stared, trying to make sense of them. Within the madly whirling cyclones she thought she glimpsed something flailing, whipping, lashing. It reminded her of a tentacled sea creatures she had seen in aquariums on her home planet.

Rallen steered the spacecraft away from the whirlpool, jetting toward the planet from which the distress signal was emanating. The spinning tentacle-like arms whirled alongside them.

"Think they're headed the same place we are?" Jeena asked nervously.

"Guess we're going to find out," Rallen said, his expression brightening.

"Hold on."

Rallen gripped the controls harder. After fully opening up the thrusters, the ship shot forward. Moments later, they hit Daichi's atmosphere.

CHAPTER THREE

It wasn't hard to figure out where the distress signal was coming from. A smoking trench in the green surface of the planet was visible from twenty miles above the planet's surface, with bits of debris and twisted metal scattered along its length. It looked as if some sort of a spacecraft had crashed there. And, judging from the smoke, it must have happened recently.

"Whoa," Rallen said, surveying the wreckage. "Not much chance we'll find survivors."

The tiny hairs on Jeena's neck stood at attention. "*Somebody* sent the signal, Rallen," she snapped.

If Rallen noticed her annoyance, he showed no sign—except for being even more cavalier as he replied, "Or some*thing*."

Daichi was a beautiful planet, famed for its rough-hewn majesty and Tabletop Mountain. Lush and green with enormous red-rock highlands, it was one of the more sparsely populated planets in the Nanairo Galaxy. Except for a couple of minor cities, the planet had few people living on it. Jeena didn't want to admit it to Rallen, but looking around, she, too, was dubious about anyone's chances of surviving a crash like that in a place like this. There were shards of luminous green metal scattered around the crash site, probably sheared from the vessel as it crashed.

"You ever see a ship made out of anything like that?" Rallen asked.

Jeena shook her head.

"Yeah, me neither."

It didn't seem like a good sign.

Rallen set the cruiser down with a flourish. Jeena had to grudgingly acknowledge that he handled the ship perfectly. Not that she'd ever admit that to him, of course. Even thinking it to herself was irritating.

They disembarked and began to scan the wreckage, searching for signs of life. Jeena activated her mavrascope, a small but complex piece of equipment she wore strapped to the back of her hand. A sensor field radiated from her outstretched palm, casting a green holo-field in the air before her. She held her breath, hoping to see the glimmer of red in the holo that would indicate the presence of some sort of life form.

Nothing.

Jeena's heart sank further. Even Rallen seemed more subdued as they poked around the smoking debris. A bird of some kind twittered nearby, then fell silent.

There were no other sounds.

Jeena scanned a piece of the ship's hull. "No markings and no galacticodes," she reported. "It doesn't look like it's from the Nanairo system."

"Probably not," Rallen replied, examining the ship's hull. "Just look at how old this thing is. It should be in Webster's museum on Kollin, not in space. In fact, that's probably why it crashed."

Rallen hauled a hunk of debris out of the wreckage, trying to hold on to the hope of finding signs of life underneath. Instead, what he found was something he'd never seen before. Lodged in the raw soil of the trench was a small

prism-shaped object made of what appeared to
be a pure white metallic substance. Unlike the
wreckage it was buried under, the prism bore not
so much as a scratch. It was perfectly intact.

He turned it over and inspected it more
closely. The gleaming white surface was broken
only by thin lines of green light that seemed to be
radiating from within. He had never seen anything
like it before, and yet there was something oddly
familiar about its shape. He slid open the paneled
console he wore on his forearm. He had always
wondered why the console had been designed
with a diamond-shaped cavity inside—a cavity
about the same size as the prism he held in his
other hand.

"Weird," he murmured. "It kinda . . . doesn't
make much sense, but it kinda looks like it fits,
whatever it is . . ."

He held the prism over the cavity and, as if
pulled by a magnetic force, the strange object

snapped into place. It fit perfectly. "Wow," he said. "Jeena, have you ever seen anything like this before?" he asked. But Jeena had moved farther down the trench, still scanning for any signs of life, and was too far away to hear him.

Her sensors had picked up a glitch over a nearby ridge. Climbing out of the trench and over a small hill, she saw what was clearly the cockpit of the spacecraft, intact despite the lethal impact of the crash. As ancient as the craft was, Jeena had to admit that its designers sure understood safety design.

Rubble from the crash lay scattered across the cockpit. Pulling off a large sheet of twisted metal, Jeena managed to uncover the cockpit's main viewport. She gasped, almost letting out a shout.

She was staring right into the face of an old man!

Jeena flinched. There were numerous deep wrinkles on the man's face, and he had an enormous, bushy beard. Taken together, they indicated that despite the long, brown hair spilling over his shoulders, he was quite old. Jeena removed a recorder from her waist belt and began to give a mission briefing. "Officer Jeena of the Nanairo Planetary Patrol responding to a distress signal that came from the planet Daichi. Officer Rallen and I have located a spacecraft near Tabletop Mountain, but no survivors have yet been found—" She stopped as the old man again caught Jeena's attention.

Examining him closer, she saw the faintest sign of his chest moving. She dropped the recorder and jumped back.

"Rallen!" she yelled. "We've got a survivor!"

Rallen's head shot up. Jeena was far enough away that he couldn't hear her words clearly, but there was no mistaking the tone of her voice. He immediately took a step in her direction. The prism on his arm glowed green.

And then from above them, the tentacles appeared.

Huge barbed strands dropped from the sky lashing out of a purple-black cyclone that hovered ominously above his head. It was one of the nasty-looking things they had encountered in space. Here, on the planet's green surface, the thing was spinning like a tornado—

The tentacles whipped back and forth, slicing the air all around Rallen. He stumbled backward, but it was no use: the vortex descended upon him and enveloped him in a sickly violet light. He was now inside it, and those lashing tentacles with the wicked-looking barbs shattered any possibility of escape.

Well, *this* wasn't covered in basic training, he thought. Maybe I could—

But there was no time to think, because he wasn't alone in the vortex. An enormous creature emerged from the gloom. It was like nothing Rallen had ever seen before anywhere in the galaxy: a towering red monster with black markings, pulsing purple, and violent whips where its arms should be. Rallen tried to find its eyes. It had none. Still, it slowly stalked straight toward Rallen, ready to strike.

And it wasn't alone. Behind it stood another one of the menacing creatures, and behind that was another, and another. Each one a different shape, but just as evil and vicious as the one before it.

Rallen gulped. "I'm an officer of the Nanairo Planetary Patrol!" he cried, calling up his identification hologram. "I order you to—" The first monster inched forward, and its shadow engulfed

Rallen and extended about five feet in every direction around him. "I—I order you to stop and put your hands—er—claws up!"

The monsters seemed unimpressed, one slightly tilting its head. The first one smashed one of its whip-arms down, barely missing Rallen and shattering the ground under him. Rallen scuttled backward.

"You're, uh . . . you're only making this harder on yourself, you know!" he shouted.

"We can do this the easy way or the hard way—it's your choice!"

Another monster slammed one of its whip-arms down and, again, Rallen barely managed to dodge it in time.

"I guess they chose the hard way," he muttered.

Rallen glanced down at the laser

blaster holstered to his hip. He had never had to use it. Rallen fired his blaster with extreme precision. His first three shots hit the creature straight-on. It barely flinched.

"Well, so much for my weapons," Rallen said. "I guess we'll have to do this the *really* hard way!"

Rallen ran through the teachings he'd received at the academy. They'd never prepared him for this—he wasn't sure anyone had ever encountered anything like this, which made training people for it kind of difficult—but he was skilled in various fighting techniques, and he knew that some would be more effective than others.

There was the neontia stance, for when your

opponent was far larger than you. Rallen looked up. *Check*. Then there was the sibelian posture, for when you weren't sure which weapons your enemy might possess. Rallen observed the tentacles. *Check*. And then there was the nielsenque, useful when you were outnumbered. Rallen counted his numerous enemies. *Check*. Oh! And then there was the—

The creatures started to surround Rallen, and the young officer didn't have any more time to consider fighting positions. Without thinking, he assumed the stakovic fighting position: one arm cocked and ready to punch, the other braced before him to shield his face from blows. Even though this whip-monster was at least twice Rallen's size, he didn't plan on going down without a fight.

At that moment, much to his surprise, the panels of his forearm console instantly slid open, and the prism he'd found began to vibrate.

Suddenly the quivering vibrations poured upward out of the prism and became a ray of blinding white light. The beam shot up and then arched back toward the ground. The light coalesced into the shape of another strange creature: a huge beast crouching on four legs, scaly green with yellow markings and small, fierce red eyes. Gigantic horns curved from either side of its head into wickedly sharp points, and the end of its tail was a round, heavy mass barbed with jutting white spikes.

"Oh, man," Rallen muttered. "I sure hope you're on my side."

He had no idea what he'd done to activate the prism. Had it been his fighting stance? His racing heart? The presence of the tentacle-vortex and the towering red monsters? Unfortunately, there was no time to think about it, because the prism was at it again. With another great beam of bright light, a second glowing beast appeared on the ground beside Rallen. This one gleamed golden and had bristly purple fur all around its wolflike snout. Its razor-sharp claws dug deep into the ground, ripping up chunks of dirt as it crouched in a fighting position. Snarling and ready to spring at any second, it looked toward the monsters.

The prism-creatures inched close to Rallen, flanking him. They roared at the red monsters. And now the prism was casting a green glow at

one end and a golden glow at its other end, the same quivering shades as the creatures on either side of Rallen. The monsters from the vortex recoiled a little.

Rallen realized that the prism had called upon some allies.

Rallen smirked. "I think my odds just got a little better," he said.

He was aware that making snap judgments about such utterly alien beings wasn't exactly a wise decision, but he'd always trusted his instincts. Besides, it wasn't like he had much choice.

He punched his fists together, psyching himself up for the fight.

"Let's do this!" he shouted, not stopping to wonder whether his new allies could understand him. "Hope you guys are good in a fight.

"Iku ze!"

His battle cry rang out above the roars and snarls of the beasts, just as the whips of the red monsters came whirling down toward him.

CHAPTER FOUR

"**R**allen!" Jeena shouted again. "Where *are* you?" She'd found what was probably the only survivor of the crash, and her partner was nowhere to be seen.

Jeena peered back through the viewport at the badly wounded man inside.

Not dead yet, she thought. But he doesn't look good.

She realized that what she'd assumed was the spacecraft's cockpit wasn't that at all. It was a cryochamber—a special compartment designed to sustain life for a long period of time at an extremely low temperature. Jeena remembered this from her science training at a bio lab back on Kollin. The technology is very similiar, she thought. But then she noticed that there was a long, wicked-looking crack snaking across the clear surface of the compartment. The cryochamber had been compromised.

"Rallen!" Jeena yelled. "Hurry up! There's a passenger here, and he's dying!"

Still no answer.

"RALLEN!"

Nothing. Jeena paused.

"Rallen?" she called again, beginning to grow worried.

Jeena turned around, hoping she could spot him, maybe just out of range of her voice. Instead, she saw the vortex. Although it was not more than two miles away, it sounded no louder than wind rustling through the ultiro grasses of her home planet.

"Rallen?" she whispered.

There was still no reply.

*I*nside the vortex, things were quite a bit louder—and more violent.

The howl of the wind made it hard for Rallen to think, and the force of the gusts turned every rock and blade of grass into deadly projectiles. The thousands of objects moving through the air at tremendous velocity made seeing even more difficult in the gloom. But Rallen knew that if he took his eyes off these enormous whip-monsters for even a moment, he was done for.

His new "partners" hadn't budged. "Maybe they're waiting for me to take the lead," Rallen said. "Great. They're three times my size, but they want me to go first. I appreciate the vote of confidence, I guess."

Rallen darted forward and immediately had to jump back, as a tentacle the size of a python smashed down onto the ground he'd been standing on a moment before.

"Whoa!" he yelled, raising his arms to shield his face from the flying debris created by the fierce blow. "Come on, you guys! ATTACK!"

The prism on his forearm vibrated, and suddenly the green and gold creatures burst into action. They lunged forward just as the whip-monster was rearing back for another blow. Rallen launched himself backward away from the whip, and the golden creature sprang past him toward the monster. It spun through the air like an Ivernies buzz saw, slicing right through one of its opponents. The whip-monster disintegrated into a puddle of ooze.

Rallen whistled appreciatively. That was one heck of an effective fighting technique, he thought to himself. But there was no time to wonder what kind of creature could turn itself into a whirling death blade. Another whip-monster was coming in for the kill—straight toward Rallen's head.

Now it was the green prism-creature's turn. It swung its tail like a massive club, knocking the monster to the ground with one powerful blow, crushing the earth beneath it.

Almost too quickly to see, the prism-creatures sliced and smashed their way through the squadron of whip-monsters. Rallen felt almost silly, standing idle in the midst of the melee with nothing to do but stay out of their way.

"I wonder if my new NPP-issued light sword has any effect against these Big Uglies," he said, studying his gauntlet, which was above the prism. A beam of white light had started to generate out of the gauntlet device. On impulse, Rallen aimed the beam of light at one of the whip-monsters and suddenly found himself holding what looked like some sort of laser sword. Rallen looked at it quickly—it had a white hilt, and its blade was made of blue light. He tried to use the sword, and to his surprise and immense pleasure, he found that the light sliced through a flailing tentacle without any hint of resistance.

"Awesome!" he crowed, slashing his newfound laser sword through the air. "I guess I have a few tricks up my sleeve as well!"

As the last red monster crashed to the ground in a pulpy mass, Rallen spun in a circle, his laser sword steady at his side, ready if needed to slash its blue light through another evildoer. The vortex shimmered

41

and dissolved. The prism-creatures leaped into Rallen's spinning beam of light, and once more the light coalesced and seemed to pour back into the prism. Suddenly, everything was quiet.

The vortex was gone, leaving only a perfectly round circle of flattened grass and a few wispy clouds.

As the dust settled, Rallen realized his new friends were gone, too, as though they'd never been there.

"Okay, that was weird," he said, breaking into a grin. "And awesome!"

Rallen looked around, dusting himself off. Jeena ran toward him.

"Rallen!" she cried. "What happened to you?"

"I was, uh . . ." Rallen paused, unsure of how to describe what had just happened. He'd never been shy about praising himself, but somehow this seemed different, and not just because it was so unbelievable. "I was just in a *battle*."

Rallen was surprised by how gratifying Jeena's reaction was. "What? Inside that vortex?" she asked.

"Yeah!" he responded. "There were these strange creatures, and a glowing light! One creature had spikes on its head and was yellow! The other had a club as a tail and was green! And it all came from this!" Rallen finally stopped speaking and held up his wrist with the prism attached to it.

Despite what she'd witnessed herself in the past few minutes, Jeena's natural skepticism—both as a scientist and as Rallen's partner—kicked in.

"Really?" She looked around pointedly as she scanned him with her mavrastrobe. "Glowing light? Strange creatures? And . . . where are they now?"

Rallen tapped his forearm console with a nonchalance he was sure would impress her.

It didn't. "Never mind, we don't have time to discuss it. I found a survivor! An old man!" Jeena cried.

"I'm not kidding, Jeena," Rallen persisted. He stumbled after her, stopping short at the sight of the bearded man in the chamber.

"Whoa! Is he still alive?"

Jeena ran another quick scan. "Yeah, but barely. He's unconscious . . . or sleeping. Or in a coma."

Suddenly the old man began to stir, moving his head and muttering. "Giorma . . . no . . . no . . . my planet—destroyed . . . Krawl coming . . . must beat the Krawl . . . must get to the Spectrobes first . . . I must find them . . . NO! Not my ship! No!"

Jeena and Rallen looked at each other, confused. The old man was making no sense.

When they turned back to him they saw that his eyes were open.

"Let's get him out of there," Jeena said calmly. Rallen leaned on the cryochamber, looking for a latch. Once again the prism on his forearm vibrated, and beneath his arm the surface of the cryochamber became streaked with green light. Then it dissolved, and the chamber was open. Whatever this prism thing is, Rallen thought, it is way too cool.

Suddenly, the old man sat up, gasping.

"The Krawl!" he croaked. "The Krawl are coming!"

CHAPTER FIVE

Jeena scanned the lone survivor for any signs of trauma he may have suffered as Rallen put a hand on his shoulder, both to try to calm him and to keep him from hurting himself. By the looks of his long, bushy brown hair and shaggy beard, it seemed that the man had been in suspended animation for a very long time, something neither officer had ever experienced but which both knew could have serious side effects.

At Rallen's touch, the man's eyes seemed

to focus for the first time. "Who . . . who are . . . ?"

"My name is Rallen, and this is Jeena. We're officers with the Nanairo Planetary Patrol. We answered your distress beacon."

The old man tilted his head. "Distress beacon?"

Oh boy, thought Rallen.

"Your ship has crashed. You're in our care now. You're safe," Jeena said gently. Rallen was amazed. He and Jeena hadn't been partners long, but he'd never heard her use that tone of voice before. It was soft and soothing, nothing like her normal sharp and scientific attitude.

But if it moved Rallen, it didn't have the same effect on the old man. "I am not safe," he replied, his voice slightly less harsh now that he was warming up. Great, Rallen thought again. He's got to be a head case, and a paranoid one at that.

The man's next words, however, made Rallen doubt his diagnosis. "*You* are not safe. No one is safe." The old man stared into Rallen's eyes, and Rallen was taken by the intensity of his gaze. "Nothing is safe until the Krawl are defeated."

Jeena and Rallen glanced at each other. *The Krawl?* Jeena's eyes asked. Rallen shrugged; he'd never heard of it either.

Rallen looked down in surprise as the old man grabbed his wrist and stared at the white prism in his gauntlet.

"Where did you get that?" the man asked.

"I found it in the wreckage." Rallen noticed that Jeena was looking at him oddly, and he turned to explain to her. "It just kinda snapped in place." Jeena looked as though she very much wanted to discuss this discovery, but Rallen saw her glance at the old man and could tell she thought they shouldn't say too much in front of him—not until they knew more.

"Well . . ." the old man said, his voice trailing off. He straightened up and for the first time seemed completely in the here and now. "You can call me Aldous. And that is a Prizmod. It controls the great Spectrobes."

Rallen studied the Prizmod as Jeena said quizzically, "The . . . Spectrobes?"

Aldous nodded. "The creatures of the light."

"I think I saw them," Rallen said. "They came out of the Prizmod when I was in the vortex."

The old man gasped. "The vortex? Here? And you were in it?" Aldous walked over to Rallen, carefully looking around and up to the sky as if another vortex was in their presence, ready to crash down upon them. "Quick! Tell me everything you saw!"

Rallen pretended to be modest. "Sure. No big deal, just me against, like, a dozen of the biggest, *nastiest* things ever. It was me and what I guess were Spectrobes against . . . something else, some kind of . . . I dunno, creatures."

"It may be hard to believe, but he's actually a really good pilot," Jeena said.

Rallen beamed. "Hey, thanks, Jeena. I—wait a second," his smile quickly leaving. "Why is that hard to believe?"

She grinned. "Because you may be the *worst* storyteller I've ever met."

Aldous wasn't amused. Nor did he think Rallen's story was far-fetched. "Those creatures you saw—those were . . . those were the Krawl, the creatures of the dark."

The smiles on Rallen's and Jeena's faces faded.

Aldous breathed, and his eyes grew distant again. "They destroyed my home planet.

50

Now they are here, in your precious Nanairo Galaxy. Every planet in this system is in grave danger. Even now, their leader plots. They speak of discovery. Of me, of the Spectrobes." His eyes focused. "A full-scale assault is coming!"

CHAPTER SIX

*I*t took nearly an hour to move all of the gear Aldous insisted they needed on their ship so he could construct his lab. Rallen initially balked, but the idea of having to explain to Commander Grant that they'd found a survivor in the wreckage but left him behind was powerful motivation. He knew Jeena thought he was just sulking over being forced to do manual labor, but actually he was despondent over having to relinquish the Prizmod.

Finally, everything Aldous wanted was on board and safely stowed away. Reluctantly, Rallen detached the Prizmod from his forearm console and held it out to Aldous. "I guess you'll be wanting this back," he said.

Aldous reached for the device and in one fluid motion performed what appeared to be a complicated maneuver using both thumbs and both forefingers.

The Prizmod opened up like a flower, revealing a glowing green and yellow interior. Aldous rapidly tapped different sections of the Prizmod, and a cylinder of translucent green light shot out of it and down to the floor. As the cylinder became transparent, Rallen could make out a small, brightly colored biped inside. Rallen's mouth dropped open as the creature, which came up to about his thigh, tentatively began to walk. The creature had a gray body, but its arms and legs—at least, Rallen assumed that's what they were—were bright yellow with blue stripes and red dots. And its red eyes seemed enormous and yet, oddly, barely open.

"Okay," Rallen said, never looking away for a moment. "I give up. What *is* this thing?"

"This is Danawa," Aldous explained. "He is a Child form of a Spectrobe. Child forms have the unique ability to search for other buried Spectrobes."

Rallen looked up. "Huh? Wait. Spectrobes are buried in the ground?"

Aldous nodded. "When they are in their fossilized state they are. And when a Spectrobe feels threatened, it will revert to its fossilized state."

"Fossilized state?"

"Yes. There are various forms and stages of Spectrobes—Child, Adult, and Evolved," Aldous explained.

"So if Rallen were a Spectrobe, he'd still be in his Child state?" Jeena asked, teasing.

Aldous ignored Jeena and went on. "There are also three different types of Spectrobes: Corona, Flash, and Aurora. Each type has its own strengths and weaknesses."

"As compared to Jeena, who doesn't seem to have any weaknesses," Rallen interjected.

Aldous sighed. "Are you two quite finished?"

The partners looked at each other and nodded. "Yes," they said together.

Aldous was about to go on when Rallen quickly added, "And she can't sing to save her life."

The old man said nothing, and the silence quickly grew oppressive. "Sorry," Rallen murmured at last.

Aldous waited, ready for another interruption from Jeena or Rallen, but none came. Finally, he went on. "As I was saying . . . there are three different types of Spectrobes—Corona, Flash, and Aurora," Aldous explained. "Corona-type

Spectrobes are at their strongest when fighting Aurora-type Krawl," he pointed out. "Aurora-type Spectrobes are best for fighting Flash-type Krawl, and Flash-type Spectrobes are most likely to defeat Corona-type Krawl."

"Uh . . ." Rallen looked at Jeena. "You're taking notes on this, right?"

Aldous's expression grew frighteningly serious. "This is no joking matter. Your life—and the lives of countless others—depends upon this."

Rallen acted as though he were about to say something in jest, but thought better of it. "Go on," he said instead.

Aldous nodded. "Thank you. Now, only Child Spectrobes have the ability to search for buried Spectrobes, but they cannot participate in a battle. Adult Spectrobes can, of course, fight in a battle but can no longer locate buried Spectrobes."

"And Evolved Spectrobes?" Rallen questioned with intensity in his voice.

"Ah, they mark the greatest point of evolution for a Spectrobe line. An Evolved Spectrobe can do everything an Adult Spectrobe can do, but they have far superior fighting skills. Then—there is the Ultimate Form, but no one has ever witnessed this. Except the Ancients."

"The Ancients?" Jeena asked with great curiosity.

"Yes," Aldous nodded. "But more on that later."

"So, Danawa here," said Rallen, gesturing at the Spectrobe who was now peering around the ship's cabin. "He's a Child Spectrobe?"

"Correct. He is going to help us find more Spectrobes."

They watched Danawa poke curiously around the ship. He doesn't look like much, Jeena thought. She looked at her partner, intending to say just that, and saw that Rallen was transfixed by the creature. Looking over at Aldous, she saw that the old man was regarding the Spectrobe with a fond gaze. She could have sworn there was at least a hint of sadness in his expression as well.

Aldous sighed and turned toward Rallen. "As for the Prizmod," he said, as though there'd been no interruption, "of course I would like it back, but what I want no longer matters. The Spectrobes are yours now."

Jeena's brow furrowed in confusion. "What?"

Rallen blinked, his unflappable demeanor pierced. "Mine? What are you talking about?"

"The Prizmod has chosen you," Aldous explained. "You, Rallen, have taken the first step toward becoming a Spectrobe Master."

Rallen stared at the older man, then looked down at the Spectrobe. Then he turned to his partner and his familiar grin broke wide open. "Hear that, Jeena?"

Jeena rolled her eyes. "Unbelievable. Because *that's* what you needed—more self-esteem."

Rallen laughed. "Okay. Let's do it."

Jeena wrinkled her brow. "Do what?"

"What do you mean 'do what?' Get Danawa to help us find more Spectrobes, silly."

Jeena started. "Now? But Commander Grant—"

"Jeena, come on!" Rallen urged. "Didn't you join the force for adventure?"

Jeena crossed her arms. "No. I joined the force because I was just hoping to be partnered with a two-year-old with no sense of duty."

Rallen slightly lowered his head, hurt by her remark.

In a softer tone of voice, Jeena added, "And who just so happens to misspell my name consistently." The pilot smiled and Jeena nodded. "Let's go."

They flew in comfortable silence for a few minutes before Rallen said, "I'm a teenager, you know."

Jeena nodded. "I know. I read your file."

Rallen turned his head toward her. "You *did*?"

"No," she laughed. "I was just kidding. But you're my partner. Of *course* I know how old you are."

"Oh," he replied. "So, uh . . . how old are you?"

"I can't believe you'd ask me that," Jeena responded. "How rude."

Rallen stammered, "Oh, really? I'm sorry, I didn't . . . I thought . . ."

"I know." Jeena laughed again. "I'm just playing with you."

Rallen looked at Jeena with newfound respect. It appeared his partner had some surprises up her sleeve.

CHAPTER SEVEN

As they made their way toward the former site of the vortex to show Aldous where it first appeared, Jeena began to regret her decision to help Rallen and Aldous. She should be making them go to the commander, check in, and get new orders. "Tell me a good reason why I'm going along with this," she said with a sigh.

Unlike Jeena, Rallen had no misgivings. He was practically skipping. "Because I asked you to," he replied.

"Right. But I said a *good* reason."

As soon as they got to the circular depression where Rallen had fought the Krawl with his new Spectrobe friends, Danawa began acting strangely. He stopped and yellow light poured out of his eyes and swept the ground like a searchlight. Suddenly, he became fixated on the ground in front of him and began jumping up and down and making what Rallen and Jeena assumed were excited noises. Either that or he was about to explode. After what they'd witnessed in the past day, it didn't seem entirely impossible.

Aldous seemed to know exactly what was going on. "That means a Spectrobe is buried here. Rallen, look at the Prizmod."

Doing as he was told, Rallen touched the Prizmod. It began to vibrate and emit what looked like Spectrobes that were surrounded by a blue glow. Then the Prizmod produced a long, thin object which resembled a pen.

"This image represents the Spectrobe buried deep within the ground," Aldous explained. "You must unearth it with that instrument in your hand, which is called a stylus."

"How?" Jeena asked.

Rallen shrugged. "Let's find out." He took the stylus and began brushing it across the hologram—as if he were gently brushing soil away. As he did, the actual ground beneath their feet started to move, and the object began to be revealed. Jeena saw that Rallen had the same intense look of concentration he sometimes—but rarely—got when trying an especially tricky maneuver while flying.

Jeena looked back down at the soil. Something

was emerging. Rallen was so focused, he didn't even notice.

"Stop!" she yelled.

Rallen blinked, his concentration broken.

"It looks like a fossil," said Jeena. She knelt to examine the strange object; it was a stone representation of a small, squat creature with large, curved horns.

"It is a Komainu," Aldous replied abruptly. His attention had been drawn to the sky. The bright afternoon had grown dim, as if a great cloud had passed over the sun. "Quickly! With the darkness comes the Krawl." Rallen looked down at his Prizmod, which was once again glowing bright.

At that moment, another massive vortex appeared and slammed into the ground, knocking them all off balance.

Rallen glanced over his shoulder. Jeena was on the ground, clutching the fossil. "Jeena, get them to the ship. I'll hold off the Krawl."

"Rallen, it's too dangerous!" Jeena objected. "Don't be a hero!"

"Ready the ship, Jeena." Rallen turned away, but before he did, Jeena noticed how grim he looked, so unlike his usual devil-may-care attitude. "Let's do this," he cried. *"Iku ze!"* And with that, he leaped into the vortex.

"Rallen is brave. But he has much to learn," Aldous observed.

Quickly turning to Aldous, Jeena snapped, "He's my partner and he's buying us time. Let's not waste it."

Picking up the Komainu fossil, she headed back to the ship. Aldous followed with Danawa.

*I*t was just as terrible being inside the vortex again as it was the first time, with the fierce wind, the deafening howl, and the legion of whip-armed monsters Rallen now knew as the Krawl. But while the vortex itself was the same, everything else was different.

Rallen moved without thinking, letting instinct and his previous experience guide him. He summoned the Spectrobes as naturally as breathing, and they sliced through the ranks of the Krawl. He fought beside them, slashing the monsters with his light sword.

"We're sending you back into the dark where you belong!" he sneered at the Krawl. Not knowing why, but trusting his gut, Rallen swiped the Prizmod and lightning cracked from above, shattering the remaining Krawl. As they were vaporized, so was the vortex. And with the vortex gone, the Spectrobes once more retreated back inside the Prizmod.

Rallen put his hands on his knees and tried to catch his breath. He'd felt strong, sure, and confident when in battle, but now that it was over, what he'd just done shook him a bit. He'd been successful twice, but these Krawl were scary things. How long would his luck hold? Deep inside, he felt a sliver of fear, though he'd never show it.

Suddenly a flash of light caused him to squint and look up. His silver ship was hovering above him. A moment later it landed next to him. Rallen whistled. "Hey, nice handling," he said softly.

"Someone told me a pilot's got to keep his skills sharp," announced Jeena, whose voice came from the ship's exterior speakers. "Know who?"

He grinned and some of the exhaustion seeped away. "I think I might have a guess. Whoever he is, he sounds smart."

Jeena lowered the rear bay door. "Jump in— there are more coming."

"I know," he said looking down at his glowing Prizmod. "Whenever those nasty Krawl are near, the Prizmod glows green!"

As Rallen started for the ramp, he glanced

up. What he saw wiped away the last traces of lethargy; there were dozens of vortexes spiraling down toward the planet's surface. "Go, go, go!" Rallen yelled, breaking into a run.

The moment his feet touched the ship, Jeena opened up the thrusters full throttle, closing the door as she did so—and just in time. The acceleration threw Rallen backward, and he was slammed against the steel doors in the back as they were still closing. Outside, vortex after vortex smashed into the ship, causing massive dents to the door as the creatures tried to destroy the NPP ship.

Rallen made his way to the bridge with difficulty, being tossed from side to side as Jeena had to avoid one vortex after another. "Some sweet steering there, partner," he said, strapping himself into his seat.

Jeena tried not to smile. "Ready to take over?" she asked. To her surprise, he wasn't.

"Nah, you got it. I'd rather just rest a bit. That is," he added, "if you don't mind."

"That's fine," she said airily, knowing as she spoke that he wouldn't be fooled by her nonchalance even for a moment.

CHAPTER EIGHT

*T*hey flew in silence for some time, each lost in their own thoughts. Soon they were out of Daichi's atmosphere—and out of harm's way.

Aldous hadn't spoken since he and Jeena had boarded the ship with the fossilized Spectrobe, but now he spoke up. "Your vessel is magnificent."

The comment surprised Jeena. True, the ship was top-of-the-line, but it was merely a patrol cruiser. There were plenty of ships in the fleet that were bigger, faster, or had more firepower. Out of the corner of her eye she noticed Rallen sit up a bit straighter.

"Hey, thanks," he said. "Yeah, she's pretty great."

Rallen turned to inspect the fossil. "This thing looks . . . dead. The Spectrobes I saw were alive and full of energy."

"And light," Aldous said, nodding. "As I mentioned, Spectrobes have many states, and the Komainu here is in its fossil form. It is how a Spectrobe protects itself when it feels threatened. At some point in the past, this one must have felt it was in some sort of danger."

"Okay. So what happens now?" Rallen questioned. "It's still in its fossilized state, so what? Does it feel it's still in danger?"

Aldous stared at the stone Spectrobe intently. "No. It knows it is safe now. But only its master can free a Komainu Spectrobe from this state."

"All right," Jeena said, trying not to sound

frustrated. If she'd been impatient with Rallen's impulsiveness, she was finding herself equally exasperated by the old man's ponderous, mysterious ways. "So free it, Aldous."

"I cannot."

Jeena gritted her teeth. "We've already set up your equipment." She gestured impatiently toward the complex lab Aldous had insisted on moving into the ship. "What more do you need?"

The old man gently ran his hands over the fossil. "It is not what *I* need—it is what a Komainu needs," he said portentously.

Jeena was determined to wait for him to explain, but Rallen spoke instead. "Its master."

Aldous straightened up. "Correct."

Jeena raised her eyebrows as she regarded her partner. "*You?*"

Rallen winked, then turned to the older man. "Just tell me how to do it, Aldous."

"But you already know."

"If I *knew* how," Rallen responded, "I wouldn't be asking."

Jeena laughed. "Rallen never asks if he already knows the answer. In fact, even if he doesn't know the answer, he usually pretends he does."

But the old man waved a hand dismissively. "He knows. He simply does not yet *know* he knows."

Jeena sighed. "So *you* know he knows even if *he* doesn't know he knows."

Aldous smiled, the sarcasm lost on him. "Precisely."

Aldous put the Komainu in a chamber of the strange lab setup that they had assembled from parts of the wreckage. "This is the incubator," he explained. "This is where you must awaken the Spectrobe from its fossilized state." He stepped back and looked expectantly at Rallen.

Rallen moved forward and squinted at the Spectrobe. What now? he thought.

"Um, wake up," he said, half joking. The

three stared at the fossil, waiting. Nothing happened. He tried again. "Wake *up*." Still nothing.

"Wake up?" he repeated, feeling silly, not to mention extremely self-conscious—a combination he was not fond of. "Come on, wake up, little guy!"

Once again, nothing.

Jeena pursed her lips. Rallen frowned. It was just like that first time in the vortex, when he'd ordered the Spectrobes to attack and they hadn't moved. What had he done to finally get them going? He couldn't remember. All he'd done was shout louder, more frantically . . .

Maybe that was it. Louder. Or had it been the intensity of his voice, the urgency?

Focusing his eyes heavily on the fossil, he took a step back and gave it one last try.

"WAKE UP!" he cried.

Suddenly, there was a brilliant flash of light.

When the light faded, where a stone statue had been a moment before there was now a living, breathing creature. A Komainu.

The Komainu whipped its head from side to side, taking in its surroundings. Then, in one tremendous leap, it jumped into Jeena's arms.

Jeena stiffened, caught off guard, then instantly melted. "Oh, he's so cute! Can I keep him?"

"Keep him? What do you feed him?" Rallen asked, confused.

"Good question, young Rallen," Aldous said, as he walked over to the side of the incubator and opened a glass door, pulling out some strange-looking rocklike figures. "These are minerals.

75

They are essentially food for the Spectrobe. These will help the Child Spectrobe grow into an Adult Spectrobe."

Rallen grabbed a mineral and examined it very closely. "So, would I buy these at, like, a mineral store at the mall on Kollin?"

"Actually, they are free. These minerals are scattered all over the surrounding planets of the Nanairo Galaxy. You can excavate minerals the same way you do with fossilized Spectrobes—by using the stylus," Aldous stated, pointing to Rallen's Prizmod.

"How many types of minerals are there?" Jeena asked.

"There are quite a few. They come in all shapes, sizes, and colors from green to gold to purple." Aldous started pulling minerals out of a cabinet that was attached to the incubator. "This one here is an Attack mineral. It looks like a pyramid. There is also the Defense mineral. They look like this," Aldous said as he held up a rectangularlike prism. "A Health mineral looks very similar to a crescent or a semicircle."

"So, once I uncover the mineral, I just drop it into the incubator and the Spectrobe will know what to do?"

"Precisely," Aldous said, placing each mineral into the incubator. The Child Spectrobe slowly walked over, sniffed one of the minerals, and swallowed it whole.

"Woah! Hungry little fella! Now, once the Child Spectrobe goes from little to Adult, what's the next step?" Rallen asked.

Aldous walked over to another area of the laboratory. He opened a drawer and pulled out a shiny silver cubelike object. "This is an Evolve Mineral." Rallen and Jeena stared in awe at the perfectly shaped mineral. "It's beautiful," Jeena said, gazing in amazement.

"Let's give it to those two Spectrobes that

fought with me and see what happens!" Rallen said.

"Not yet Rallen." responded Aldous, his demeanor quickly turning serious. "You only use the Evolve Mineral when you need it the most. Right now is not that time. But that time will come. Soon enough." He walked over and placed the Evolve Mineral in Rallen's hands. "And when that time comes, you will need to give this to the Spectrobe."

Rallen nodded, knowing that now was no time to crack a joke.

"You can place it in your Prizmod," added Aldous.

There was a moment of silence, which was quickly broken by the Komainu as it purred in Jeena's lap.

She rubbed her cheek against the Komainu's. "Okay, how big will he get? Tell the truth."

"He'll get bigger. Much, *much* bigger," Aldous

replied, growing serious again. "As for the truth? There are many truths yet to be revealed."

He turned and gazed out of a portal. "Even now, an armada, a vortex of unimaginable power, hunts us." He turned back to Jeena and Rallen. "The Krawl. All in their path will be destroyed, every planet, your planet . . . this entire galaxy."

He turned and regarded them again. "Unless we stop them. And our only hope is the Spectrobes." He directed his gaze at Rallen.

"And you."

CHAPTER NINE

"And that's what we found, sir," Jeena said, finishing her report. They were back on their home planet, Kollin, in the Planetary Patrol Headquarters. They'd dropped the ship off to be repaired with Maxx, the chief mechanic, and headed immediately for the briefing room. As they walked, Jeena shuddered. She couldn't help but think of the destruction that might be taking place back on Daichi, particularly if all those vortexes had descended upon the planet. She was glad it was sparsely populated. Hopefully, the vortexes would not touch down near a settlement.

All too soon they found themselves in the briefing room, with Commander Grant at the front. As Jeena and Rallen filled him in, Grant rubbed his chin with a fist, staring off into the distance. "Hmm," he murmured, then turned to look at Jeena. "What do you make of this, Jeena?"

She was tempted to glance over at her partner, but she held the commander's gaze. He had asked for *her* opinion. "The Krawl we encountered exhibited characteristics much like those of Category Five threat intruders." She paused, aware that Rallen was not going to like what she had to say next. "I think—I think we may need assistance from the Special Forces team."

She had been right. Rallen forgot to stand at attention as he whirled to face her, his expression furious. "What?" he practically screamed. Then, realizing he might be out of line, Rallen turned to face Commander Grant again, once more at attention. "We don't need them, sir. I'm sure I can handle the Krawl with the Spectrobes. Besides," he added, shooting Jeena a meaningful glare, "we don't even know if the Special Forces weapons are effective against the Krawl. My laser blaster was useless."

Jeena knew that a bond had finally been forming between her and Rallen. She'd always imagined—and indeed been told—that partners would bond, but she and Rallen hadn't come close to that before. However, the pressure of standing up to the Krawl—not to mention the sheer adventure—had brought them much closer together. Jeena knew that what she was about to say would seriously jeopardize their new relationship. But the stakes were too high. She felt she had no choice.

"It's not their weapons I'm counting on, Rallen," she said. "It's their training and experience. Aren't you always going on about the superior skills of Special Forces? Don't you *want* to work with them on this?"

Although hurt by his partner's apparent lack of faith in him, Rallen had to admire the skill with which Jeena presented her argument. Rallen had no choice but to admit defeat. His shoulders sagged and he sighed heavily.

Commander Grant studied the partners. Despite the urgency of the situation, the commander remained cool and methodical, taking his time with decisions and never appearing to feel rushed in any way.

Rallen and Jeena weren't quite so calm. They'd faced the Krawl personally, and although they'd never say so out loud, they felt that perhaps their commander didn't fully recognize the gravity of the situation.

"Rallen," Commander Grant finally said, "I'm going to provide you clearance for Special

Forces equipment on this investigation—we've got more than a few weapons that have been under wraps for some time. Perhaps this is just the opportunity to move beyond the testing stage and see how they really perform in the field. You'll be assigned a comprehensive set, but here's one I want you to familiarize yourself with immediately." The commander pointed to a gleaming white weapon with bright green trim. "Its code name is Palaceo."

Rallen lifted the Palaceo. "It looks like a type of blaster," he said, running his fingers over the cool steel.

"It is," the commander said, removing the gun from Rallen's hand; the way the young pilot was almost bouncing the weapon, getting used to its weight, made everyone nearby nervous. "It operates by cold fusion and, I suspect, might have more success against the Krawl than your normal weapons."

"Except for that laser sword," Rallen said.

"That thing cut through those Krawl like a knife through butter!"

"Ah yes," Commander Grant nodded, "the Sword of Light. This is part of that same weapons project. If you enjoyed the sword, wait till you see the Palaceo in action."

Rallen and Jeena both wondered if the commander had been listening to her report. He hadn't seen the Krawl and didn't seem to have really understood just how extreme an enemy they were facing. Without any firsthand evidence, what could possibly possess the commander to make a sweeping statement like that? There was no time to express such a sentiment, even if either of them had dared. Commander Grant continued, "I want you to set out immediately to make clear the identity of this enemy."

"Understood," Rallen said. Jeena knew that whatever doubts her partner might have shared with her, he was pleasantly surprised at this turn of events—a full battery of brand-new Special Forces weapons. She was *not* looking forward to the gloating that was sure to come. If there was one thing Rallen was even better at than flying, it was boasting; he'd raised it to an art form. And it looked as if, in this case anyway, he would have an awful lot of material to work with.

"And I'm also assigning the Special Forces team to this new threat." Commander Grant said.

They both turned toward him in surprise.

"Huh?" Rallen blurted out. A flicker in the commander's eyes showed that he'd noticed the improper response from the pilot, and that he was going to overlook it—this time. Commander Grant turned to Jeena. "Jeena, go ahead and transmit all the data you have on this case to Special Forces. We'll integrate their findings into our file and ask the forensics division to analyze all the data."

Jeena nodded. "Yes, sir." Now it was her turn to give her partner a small self-satisfied smile. He shook his head in disgust. Not being able to rub Jeena's face in his triumph didn't take away the thrill of being able to access Special Forces equipment . . . but it took a bit of the luster off.

The monitors behind the commander flickered. There was no place in the entire Nanairo Galaxy more advanced and secure, so any sign of instability—even one as minute as a screen flicker—put Jeena and Rallen instantly on edge.

Commander Grant didn't appear concerned, although he did seem intrigued as he moved closer to inspect the monitors. After one step, he stumbled as the floor beneath their feet began to sway. Jeena put her arms out for balance, and even Rallen had to bend his knees and assume a semicrouching position to withstand the rocking movement.

The motion ceased almost immediately.

"Maybe the drive needs to be stabilized," Jeena suggested. "Perhaps we should—"

That was as far as she got. Suddenly, the station itself seemed to shred open like a tin can, as a giant black vortex descended into the briefing room.

Razor-sharp, barbed-wirelike spikes whipped from the center of the vortex, slicing though the outer walls. Jeena and Rallen fell backward just in time, barely avoiding being cut in two.

Rallen immediately assumed a battle position, readying the Prizmod for a fight. Out of the howling whirlwind emerged a Krawl. Rallen glanced down at the Palaceo he was holding and decided there was no time like the present to use it. Unsure of the power it possessed, Rallen quickly, but carefully, aimed and fired a blast at the Krawl's right shoulder.

The impact spun the creature around. When it faced Rallen again, it lurched to the side, obviously wounded. Another blast knocked it back into the large, violent whirlpool of the vortex, and it didn't return.

But something even worse did.

Even after their experiences with the Krawl, Rallen and Jeena had trouble wrapping their heads around just how large this creature was. And even beyond size, the Krawl radiated a sort of primitive evil that neither Rallen nor Jeena previously imagined existed.

But this new creature made them forget all about the first Krawl. Rather than the immense red and black demon Rallen had battled twice, this time they faced an even larger one—black with pulsing purple and red ooze coming from within.

Its tentacle-like limbs ended in huge, round, spike-studded clubs. It took a step, shattering the ground beneath it.

Rallen shook his head, trying to clear his mind

and prepare for another fight. But the Krawl ignored him. Instead, it turned and faced Commander Grant.

The commander threw his shoulders back and stood his ground. For a few seconds, the two stared at each other. Then, with a hiss and a roar, the Krawl disappeared into the vortex, and then the vortex vanished.

Jeena and Rallen looked around. The ceiling

and walls, which they could have sworn had just been ripped to pieces, were utterly untouched. There were no signs that the vortex had ever been in the station at all, much less in this room.

"*Wha?*" Rallen stuttered.

"I—" Jeena stammered.

They looked to their superior officer, who calmly dusted off his sleeves and straightened his lapels, then turned toward them as though nothing had happened.

While his usual deliberate manner was still there in the sound of his voice, what he said conveyed an unmistakable air of determination: "I believe you two have your orders. The new Special Forces weapons should have already been loaded on your ship by now. I suggest you get back to Daichi while there's still a Daichi to get back to."

Without a word, the partners spun around and raced for their ship.

Alone in the briefing room, Commander Grant sat down slowly. He stared into the space in front of him, focusing on nothing.

"The Krawl . . ." he said breathlessly.

CHAPTER TEN

*T*he distance from the briefing room to the landing bay where the ship was docked was normally a brisk ten-minute walk. Jeena and Rallen covered it in five.

Maxx and her assistant mechanics jumped out just as Rallen and Jeena ran up.

"Dunno what the rush is," one of them said, but the partners ran past without even a glance and immediately shut the door.

"She's all ready!" the chief mechanic yelled,

then turned to her assistant. "Space jockeys. They think they're so important. But where would they be without us, huh?" Maxx puffed out her cheeks impatiently. "Stranded on some asteroid, most likely, that's where."

Jeena's voice rang through the intercom. "Maxx! Sorry for the rush! Thanks so much for fixing the ship. She feels good as new! Right, Rallen?"

From the cockpit of the ship, Rallen yelled, "Maxx! You're the best! I give the ship two thumbs-up! Now 'scuse us while we go handle some NPP business!"

Maxx looked at her assistant and said with slight embarrassment, "Okay. Maybe I spoke too soon."

Her assistant eyed her. "Hmph, right."

Jeena was still strapping herself in when Rallen lifted off and immediately banked. He gunned the engines to escape velocity, and moments later the blue sky turned into the blackness of space. As always, the brightness and clarity of the stars took Jeena's breath away. Even now, she was entranced. Because now she knew her beautiful and loving world was threatened—a thought almost too terrible to consider. She shuddered. What if they were too late to save Daichi?

"It would be a horrific tragedy were Daichi to fall, would it not?" a voice asked.

Jeena gasped and Rallen jumped. They both spun around in their seats to see Aldous.

"What . . . how . . . when?" Rallen sputtered.

Some of the incredible tension of the previous twenty minutes drained away, and Jeena found herself giggling at her partner's uncharacteristic stammering.

"My questions exactly," she managed to say.

"It is simple," the old man responded. "When the Krawl attacked your headquarters, I knew you two, as the only ones on the force with the proper experience, would be detailed to engage them again. Either that or, I assumed, you would take it upon yourselves to do so. Perhaps I misread your characters in our brief but . . . intensive . . . time together?"

Silence hung in the air until Rallen suddenly said, "Hey, wait a second . . . how did you know the Krawl attacked HQ? Was it visible from outside the briefing room?"

"You depend too much on your eyes, young Rallen. There are more things in this universe than those which we can simply see." Aldous smiled. "That, and I stayed on the ship to keep Danawa company." He rubbed Danawa's head as Jeena and Rallen looked on. Their perfect moment wouldn't last long.

"I can see Daichi in thrusting range." Jeena said. Her voice was low and solemn as she pointed in front of her. From space, there was no sign of the dozens of evil vortexes the young officers had seen spinning toward the planet when they had made their escape a short time ago. All of the vortexes must have touched down, and who knew what havoc they were wreaking on the beautiful second planet of the Nanairo Galaxy? And if the Krawl succeeded in destroying Daichi, which planet would be next?

"I don't understand," Rallen muttered. "Why pick on a planet like Daichi? It's peaceful, it doesn't have many natural resources, the population is small, and it is not threatening to anyone. I don't get it."

"That is because you do not have enough experience with the Krawl," Aldous said in a serious tone. "Not yet." In a quieter voice, Aldous added, "Let us hope you are able to live long enough to gain more."

"Thanks, friend—I appreciate the pep talk," Rallen said sarcastically. "So you've got a ton of experience with the Krawl; how's about you fill us in on what they're doing?"

"They are setting a trap." Aldous clasped his hands behind his head and continued. "They now know there is a new Spectrobes Master, and they can tell he is gifted . . . but barely tested. They hope to capitalize on your lack of experience, Rallen. Put simply, they are planning to rid themselves of you before you become an expert."

Rallen swallowed. That was not encouraging. "Okay," he said. "Switching gears. How about you tell me a few things. You know, to help me along toward total, uh, masterdom."

"That is one of my duties," Aldous confirmed.

"Great. So the two Spectrobes who fought with me in the vortex—what are they? Do they have names?"

"From your description, you must have encountered Spikan and Zozane. Spikan is an Aurora Spectrobe, and Zozane is a Corona Spectrobe."

"Right. And they're obviously not Child forms, so I guess they were . . . Adults?"

"Correct. And as impressive and invaluable as they were, they will be even more so when they attain their Evolved form. You will then know them not as Spikan and Zozane, but as Spikanor and Zozanero—Evolved Spectrobes!"

"Well, evolved or not, and ready or not, here we come," Rallen replied as they entered Daichi's atmosphere. "And by 'ready,' I mean whether *I'm* ready or not."

Jeena was relieved to see he was grinning. And if she could tell that there was a small flicker of uncertainty in her partner's eyes, she did not betray her thoughts.

When they got closer, they could see no sign of the Krawl within sixty yards of their initial battle. "Could they be lying in wait?" Jeena asked.

"Good question," Rallen said. "And, hey, Aldous, you're the expert, so you should be able to tell us—what *was* that thing back at HQ? It was a Krawl, I'd swear, but it looked nothing like the one I fought earlier here on Daichi."

Aldous nodded gravely. "Yes. Based on the description that was one of the Evolved Krawl. Terrible as the regular Krawl are, the Evolved Krawl are that much worse. Much, much worse. They can command the Krawl and have all their abilities . . . and more. They can blend in with any environment, any surrounding. They can also . . . there!" Aldous exclaimed, breaking off his thought.

Rallen and Jeena had been transfixed by Aldous's words, trying to imagine something— anything—worse than the beasts Rallen had faced. Aldous's shout brought them back to the present, and they looked where his finger was pointing.

What they saw horrified them. A swarm of vortexes were attacking Perfuz, Daichi's largest city.

Rallen brought the ship in low—for if a vortex

managed to slam it to the ground, he wanted to be at a low enough altitude that the crash wouldn't necessarily be fatal . . . although he was going to do his best to avoid any sort of crash at all.

"Jeena, take over," he said, unbuckling himself.

"What are you doing?" she asked, grabbing the controls immediately.

"I'm not sure yet," Rallen replied, grinning. "I'll let you know when I figure it out."

"Rallen—" Jeena began, but he laughed.

"I'm just kidding, Jeena. I want you to fly right through one of those vortexes."

Jeena didn't take her eyes off their destination as she yelled, "What!? Rallen, this is no time for jokes!"

Rallen smiled. "No joke, partner. I want to hit 'em fast, and I want to hit 'em hard. They think I'm an easy mark?" Rallen grabbed the Palaceo blaster and turned to look at Aldous, his smile never wavering. "Well, I'm gonna show 'em something they ain't never seen."

Jeena opened her mouth to object, but then had a change of heart. "Let's do this thing," she said.

"I'm going to drop out of the hatch the second we pierce the vortex wall. You'll need to shut it immediately or—"

"—or we'll probably get pulled out after you," Jeena responded. "I may not be the hottest young pilot in the Nanairo Planetary Patrol, but even so, I know my basic physics, thanks."

"Oh, I don't think anyone's ever doubted that. Just, you know, trying to make sure at least some of us make it back."

"What, are you kidding me again?" she asked, with only a slight hitch in her voice. "We're going to be celebrating over some jumbo Fifty-niner burgers in the officers' club tonight."

"Sounds good to me," Rallen smiled. "You

know what a sweet tooth I've got. Okay, we're about to hit. Oh, and I'm totally maxed out at the club, so you're buying!"

With that, Rallen slammed his fist on the hatch button. It slid open instantaneously, and he got sucked into the void.

The ship's tail slid sideways as the vessel got caught in the whirlwind. Against all instinct and training, instead of steering in the direction of the tail, Jeena turned against it, whipping the ship into an uncontrollable spin. Aldous moaned, and Jeena nearly blacked out from the bone-crushing G-forces.

And then they were back out of the vortex. The ship was still spinning, faster than Jeena had ever experienced. She pulled the nose up, then immediately pushed it back down and then up once more. The violent motions were sickening, but each time she moved the nose she increased the air resistance and slowed the craft slightly.

After a dozen such moves she decreased the rate of spin just enough that she was able to pull out and level off.

Jeena caught her breath, then started to scout for likely locations to land. After what had just occurred, she wanted to try to check the ship out before they left the atmosphere again. Thank goodness I thanked Maxx before we left, she thought. Her hands are going to be full when we get back!

"What do you think?" Jeena asked the old man, who still had his eyes squeezed shut. "Think they've ever seen *that*?"

Aldous was breathing heavily now and didn't respond. Jeena was starting to worry that the day's events—particularly those in the last two minutes—were too much for the old man, especially when he said, "I think . . . I think you are starting to sound something like your partner."

Meanwhile, down in the vortex, Rallen found he'd hit the ground with far less force than he'd anticipated. He had kept the ship low so the fall wouldn't be fatal, but with the wind there was no guarantee of that. But rather than magnify the plunge, the wind that was spinning in an upward direction had actually cushioned the descent.

He didn't have time to get his bearings, however. His feet had barely touched the ground when the Krawl emerged.

Rallen immediately activated the Prizmod and was joined again by his old allies, Spikan and Zozane. "All right, guys—as Jeena would say, let's do this thing. *Iku ze!*"

Utilizing the new Palaceo blaster, Rallen went to work with Spikan and Zozane, at times on their own and sometimes as a team. If they'd been amazing fighters the first time, now that Rallen had a better idea of the Spectrobes' capabilities—and his own—they were something else entirely. At times it felt less like fighting and more like an elaborate dance . . . though with potentially deadly risks.

Four, five, six Krawl struck out at them at once, but Rallen and the Spectrobes beat them all back.

Still, the creatures of the dark kept coming. And coming. Rallen was getting tired. And though he couldn't be sure, he had an idea that the Spectrobes were starting to feel the same way.

"Well, Jeena," he said to himself. "Looks like dessert is *definitely* on you. The upside is, at least it's only going to cost half as much."

Rallen blasted another Krawl back into the vortex. "Looks like I really wasn't quite as ready as I thought. And obviously not as evolved."

Something clicked when he realized what he had just said. But he didn't have time to contemplate it now. He turned just in time to see a Krawl behind him, a sharp tentacle raised, about to smash him into oblivion. Rallen fell to the ground, blasting as he went. The Krawl vaporized into a fine black dust, but there was another foul creature right behind the one he had just destroyed.

"That's it!" Rallen yelled. "Evolve . . . evolve!" He turned toward the Spectrobes, who were busy trying to hold their own Krawl at bay. The Spectrobes were barely visible as dozens of Krawl moved in on Spikan and Zozane, smothering them in a mass of tentacles and blackness. "I need you guys to evolve! It'd be nice if I knew how you do that," he said nervously. Then he remembered. "That's it! They need the Evolve Mineral!"

The Spectrobes were now completely submerged by the Krawl. Rallen opened a compartment in the Prizmod and pulled out the shiny cubelike mineral. Dodging a blow from another one of the creatures, Rallen rolled, then got up on one knee, threw the mineral toward Spikan and Zozane, and summoned his deepest, most urgent command. "*Evolve.*"

There was a flash of light. Any Krawl that had been around the Spectrobes disintegrated or was pushed back fifty feet. The blinding light died down, and there before him stood creatures Rallen knew instantly as Spectrobes; but they were different from the ones he'd been fighting alongside. Spikan and Zozane—or Spikanor and Zozanero, as he recalled Aldous telling him—were nearly double the size they had been before. Spikanor's horns and claws were bigger still, and looked far sharper and more threatening, while Zozanero appeared to have acquired an entire mane of deadly spikes. But as amazing as these differences were, there was something else different about them, something Rallen couldn't quite put his finger on—and now, he realized, wasn't the time to be thinking about such things.

Rallen wasted no more time pondering this unexpected gift. "*Attack!*" he commanded the Spectrobes.

They did. Spikanor and Zozanero fell upon the Krawl like waves crashing upon a shore. The Krawl were tossed aside and quickly fell back like a deck of cards. Within moments, the Krawl were either defeated or in full retreat.

Scarcely fifteen seconds later, the vortex vanished. But there were still a dozen other vortexes waiting for a taste of these new, evolved heroes.

The Spectrobes immediately rushed into another vortex, but within seconds it also vanished, and before the Spectrobes could attack a third time, all the remaining vortexes departed from the planet.

Rallen dropped to his knees with exhaustion. When he looked up, the Spectrobes were gone as well.

With considerable difficulty, Rallen raised his

head and saw Jeena jumping out of the ship.

"For a second there, I thought you were trying to get out of joining me for dessert," Jeena said.

"You see right through me," he said heavily. "I just didn't quite know how to tell you."

Jeena helped him to his feet. Rallen took a step toward the ship and stumbled. She caught his arm and slung it over her shoulder. "It's okay," she said. "You can lean on me." And with that, Rallen passed out in Jeena's arms.

CHAPTER ELEVEN

"We're here. Rallen. *Rallen*!"

Rallen awoke with a start. Had it all been a dream?

"I guess fighting the Krawl really takes a lot out of you, huh?" Jeena asked.

Rallen looked around and saw that he was on the ship—and if Jeena's words weren't enough to convince him it hadn't been a dream, the sight of Aldous was. "Wow. I crashed hard."

"I'll say. You were snoring before we even buckled you in."

"Yeah?" He looked down and noticed he was securely strapped in.

"Aww . . . you care," he said in a baby voice.

"You must still be dreaming," Jeena said, rolling her eyes. "I just didn't want to get docked if there was a safety inspection."

They headed into HQ, but as they passed Maxx, Jeena asked her to give the ship an extrathorough going-over. "I'm not sure what the ship's maximum revolutions per second are, but I think we probably tripled them today." Maxx seemed unsure as to whether or not Jeena—of all people in the patrol—was pulling her leg.

As they entered the briefing room, Rallen noticed that the old man was with them this time. Last time he'd simply vanished along the way, and neither Jeena nor Rallen had noticed when or where to. "Uh, Aldous . . . look, no offense, you've been really great—in fact, I don't know how we would have gotten through today without you. But this is for officers only and—"

"—I will stay," Aldous replied firmly.

Rallen looked at Jeena, who shrugged. Yesterday, the idea of bringing an unauthorized visitor into the briefing room would have gone against her play-by-the-book attitude. Now it was perhaps the least remarkable part of the entire day.

Commander Grant looked up as they entered. "Congratulations on a job well done," he said. "The people of Perfuz are more than a little grateful. As I understand it, we've received more than ten thousand thank-you letters already."

Jeena blushed, but Rallen scoffed. "No thanks necessary, sir. All in a day's work."

"Mmm," Commander Grant said, turning his gaze toward Aldous.

"Oh, sir," Jeena quickly said. "This is Aldous. He's the survivor we found in the wreckage on Daichi. Aldous, this is our commanding officer, Commander Grant."

The two men looked at each other in silence, then both nodded slowly.

"Aldous," Commander Grant said.

"Grant," Aldous said back.

Rallen and Jeena looked at each other out of the corners of their eyes.

An aide rushed into the room and handed the commander something. He looked at it, then turned to the officers. "All in a day's work, I believe you said, Rallen. The day's not over quite yet—nor, apparently, is your work. The Krawl have been spotted approaching the lava planet, Genchi. You'd better get going."

Rallen and Jeena saluted quickly, then ran from the room.

As they sprinted toward their ship, Maxx said,

"Hey, she's in perfect condition, but I checked the instruments and . . . what did you *do* to her?"

Jeena yelled, "You'd never believe me if I told you, Maxx—or, if you did, you'd never let me fly a ship again!"

The partners buckled up and Rallen gunned the engine. Destination: space.

"Now it looks like *you're* trying to get out of buying the first dessert," Rallen said.

Jeena smiled and shook her head as she programmed the computer to give them as much information as possible about the specific area of Genshi where the Krawl were spotted. "Can't put anything over on you," she said.

"You know it." Rallen laughed. "So. What do you say? Should we do this thing?"

Jeena pointed toward Genshi. "*Iku ze!*" she yelled.

THE STORY OF THE SPECTROBES CONTINUES IN RISE OF THE ANCIENT . . .

Rallen and Jeena continue their quest across the galaxy to discover more buried Spectrobes and put an end to the evil force known as the Krawl. But the Spectrobes are not the only discovery occurring in the Nanairo Galaxy. An ancient set of ruins have been uncovered on Planet Nessa. When Rallen and Jeena team up with Professor Kate, a scientist from Kollin, the clues they find at the ruins are more than they could ever imagine. Could the ruins actually be an ancient machine somehow linked to the creatures of the light? As our heroes try to find answers, a dark being known only as Jado is trying to find them. Find out what happens in *Spectrobes: Rise of the Ancient!*